This book belongs to

For my baby girl. Always love the skin you're in.
Keilly

For Towa.
Cosei

American edition published in 2017 by Lantana Publishing Ltd., London.
www.lantanapublishing.com

First published in the United Kingdom in 2016 by
Lantana Publishing Ltd., London.
info@lantanapublishing.com

Text © Keilly Swift 2017
Illustration © Cosei Kawa 2017

Distributed in the United States and Canada by Lerner Publishing Group, Inc.
241 First Avenue North
Minneapolis, MN 55401 USA

For reading levels and more information, look for this title at www.lernerbooks.com.

Printed and bound in Hong Kong.
Cataloguing-in-Publication Data Available.

ISBN-13: 978-1-911373-16-2
eBook ISBN: 978-1-911373-19-3

The Tigon and the Liger

Keilly Swift & Cosei Kawa

LANTANA PUBLISHING

Tyler the tigon was terribly rare.

A big cat like him isn't found everywhere.

Unique from his **ears** to his **tail** to his **tum**,

his dad was a **TIGER**, a **LION** his mom.

No one would play with him – all made a fuss.

"Buzz off!" roared the tigers. **"You're not one of us!"**

"You're small!" said the lions. "Your fur isn't right!"

"You need a big mane and a much stronger bite!"

He said to himself, **"Am I really that bad?**

Or is it that tigons are meant to be sad?

I'll go somewhere else, somewhere far, far away!

No one will miss me – I'll set off today!"

He walked...

and he walked...

and he walked a bit more.

He just kept on walking

till his paws were sore.

I'm safe now,

thought Tyler.

A feline-free zone!

But just then

he realized

he wasn't alone...

Lyla the liger was terribly rare.

A big cat like her isn't found everywhere.

Unique from her **ears** to
her **tail** to her **tum**,

her dad was a **LION**,
a **TIGER** her mom.

The lions ignored her
and said, **"Go away!"**

The same from the tiger cubs
day after day.

They shouted, **"You're big and your fur is all wrong!**

Your roar is too weak and your tail is too long!"

Lyla thought no one
on earth understood,

but Tyler the tigon
was someone who could!

The cats shared their tales
and began to have fun.

Their games

were for

TWO

now,

instead of

just one!

Tyler loved
hiding because
he was small,

and Lyla loved
climbing because
she was tall.

The best thing of all was they finally saw...

being different
was **special**, it
wasn't a flaw.

Together they shouted, **"It's time to go home.
We'll both face the others but now, not alone!"**
They walked and they walked and they walked a bit more,
too happy to realize that their paws were sore.

Before long they noticed

some big cats were near.

A lion walked by

with a *snarl* and a *sneer*.

"Ha ha!" chuckled Lyla, and Tyler laughed too.
"We love being different, we honestly do!"

The day after that
something startling
occurred.

A tiger came over and asked for a word...
He looked a bit nervous,
but said with a smile,

**"Your game looks just great
– can I play for a while?"**

News of all this must have spread like wildfire, as soon a young lion came there to inquire....

"**Ahem,**" he coughed, shyly,
"**your game looks quite fun.**

**I'd love to play, too,
if you've got room for one!**"

Soon **hundreds** of big cats had joined in the game.

None cared who was different or who was the same.

They now knew it matters

not one little jot,

who's **big**
or who's small,

who has

stripes or

has spots.

And that goes for

zebras

and donkeys

and bears,

kangaroos,

wallabies,

horses

and hares.

For zedonks

and zorses

and all wallaroos,

pumapards,

leopons,

and most of all...

YOU!

Just know you're unique in your own special way.

Remember what Tyler and Lyla would say...

With straight hair or curly, and brown eyes or blue,

love the skin you're in – there's no one like you!